To my Princess Party . . . Princess Beverly,
Princess Angela and Princess NataLee.
To Grand Princess Rachel and Grand Princess Mabel Joy.

To the Creative Princesses Nancy, Ronnie and Cecilia,
who helped so much to make this book.

Most especially, to my daddy . . . I was always his Princess.

ISBN 978-0-545-32853-1

Copyright © 2009 by Joy Allen.
All rights reserved. Published by Scholastic Inc., 557 Broadway, New York, NY 10012,
by arrangement with G. P. Putnam's Sons, a division of Penguin Young Readers Group,
a member of Penguin Group (USA) Inc. SCHOLASTIC and associated logos
are trademarks and/or registered trademarks of Scholastic Inc.

12 11 10 9 8 7 6 5 4 3 2 1   11 12 13 14 15 16/0

Printed in the U.S.A.   40

This edition first printing, January 2011

Design by Marikka Tamura
Text set in Alghera Bold
This book was created in traditional watercolor and pencil, then digitally enhanced.

Princess Party

JOY ALLEN

Please Come

SCHOLASTIC INC.
New York Toronto London Auckland
Sydney Mexico City New Delhi Hong Kong

A Princess is pretty
in pink, red or green

A Princess is perfect
in dresses or jeans

A Princess is posh in boots or high heels

She likes to dress up

and show how she feels

A Princess can twirl

A Princess can whirl!

A Princess is such an incredible girl!

A Princess is pleased when her friends come to stay

It is grand to have pals to play with all day

Puffy pink ponies are proper to ride
Carriages take the procession outside

Defend the castle

Dance at the ball

Plan a tea party—these girls do it all!

Till it's time to take boots and beads
off for the night

Read a fabulous story

and turn off the light

And in their dreams . . .

Princesses twirl

Princesses whirl

For Princesses are incredible girls!